This book is dedicated to everyone
who works to keep hearts healthy:
the big ones and small ones, the sick ones
and well ones, the lost ones and found ones.

The Little Girl Who **Found** Her Heart

Story by David Gehrke

Design by Betsy Alvarez

Illustration by Nick Guarracino

There was a girl named Sally Smart
Who did not think she had a heart.
The thought first came to her the day

Her sense of rhythm went away.

She could not drum, or tap her feet,
Or snap her fingers to the beat.

So one day little Sally Smart

Said,
"It's time for me to find my heart!"

She wrote a note and packed a pack
And started down the dusty track.

It's time
for me to find
my heart.
— SALLY

Soon, Sally met a friendly cat.
"Do you know where my heart is at?"

He winked and said, "No, not today…
But do you like to

run and play?"

"Of course!"

said Sally with a smile.

And they ran and skipped and played a while.

Next, Sally met a jolly toad.
"Have YOU seen my heart along this road?"
"Nope," he said, then gave a croak…

"Would you like to hear a funny joke?"

"You bet!" said Sally with a grin,

And
she couldn't keep her laughter in.

Then Sally met a buzzing bee.

"Do you know where
my heart might be?"

...And she ran into the woods to hide.

She climbed a tree and shed a tear.
"I'll never find my heart up here!

I asked the cat, the toad, and bee
But **no one knew where it might be!**"

It was there she met a wise old owl
Who fixed her with his wisest scowl.

"Oh, Mr. Owl, might you know…
Where oh where did my heart go?"

"I know you think you have no heart

But let me tell you, Sally Smart…

"You told the toad
you like to laugh

"You told the cat you like to play
And run and skip and jump all day.

No matter what
the joke or gaffe.

"You told the bee you
fear his sting
And fear can be a healthy thing.

"All these things (which seem apart),
Together mean

you HAVE a heart!"

"You're right!"
exclaimed Miss Sally Smart.

"All this time I HAD a heart!

And though I couldn't tap my feet
My heart, it seems, has kept the beat."

And that's the tale of Sally Smart
The little girl who found her heart.

The people who created this little book:

David Gehrke lives in New York City, where he is an advertising writer.

Betsy Alvarez lives in New York City, where she is an advertising art director.

Nick Guarracino lives in Norwalk, Connecticut and works in New York City, where he is an illustrator and advertising art director.

Glenn Batkin and **Chris Palmer** also work in advertising. They provided overall creative direction and helped Dave, Betsy, and Nick out in any way they could.

This is their first children's book.

This book is a work of heart. And it was brought to life by an advertising agency called **Cline Davis & Mann** (CDM, for short).

CDM works exclusively in healthcare. And we are privileged to work with companies who develop medicines that help millions of people all over the world keep their hearts healthy. We're also proud partners of organizations that tirelessly raise awareness about the importance of heart health.

This book comes from our hearts. We hope it will find a place in yours.

All proceeds from the sale of this book
will be donated to charitable organizations.